The Old Tree

Book One

Tricia Martin

The Old Tree Series

Book One
The Old Tree

Book Two
The Land of Bizia

Book Three
The Kingdom of Knon

Book Four
The Mild, Mild West

Book Five
Into the Night Sky

Book Six
The Arabian Lights

Book Seven
One for All and All for One

To Michael
Because of your love for reading,
especially fantasy adventures,
this series is dedicated to you.
Someday you will give these stories
to your own children to read,
and that will make me laugh
with joy.

Contents

The Old Tree

Book One

Tricia Martin

Chapter One

The New Neighbor

Summer vacation had started, and Mike ran excitedly through the park, finally arriving at the tree.

There it stood, larger than life, with vibrant green leaves that seemed to glow and a trunk the most unusual brown, alive with energy.

On rare occasions, a gap would appear, inviting Mike to crawl inside. He wondered if the gap would appear now.

Standing in front of the tree, he suddenly felt someone's eyes on the back of his head.

Turning around, he was startled by a tall man stepping out from behind another tree. The man approached him, glowing with a strange light, and smiled, but it wasn't a nice smile. Mike felt drawn to the glowing man, but fear filled him when he looked into the stranger's cold eyes.

"Hello there." The stranger extended his hand in a friendly gesture, but Mike stepped back.

The stranger continued. "I noticed you studying that tree. I'm interested in it as well. My name is Sitnaw, and I'm not from your world. But I see you've already experienced something otherworldly, haven't you?" Now his voice became commanding and harsh. "Tell me about the tree."

Mike instinctively backed away as the man reached out a hand to grab him, and then he turned around and ran. When he looked back, the man had vanished, but he kept on running.

He stopped and quickly looked behind him again. The stranger was nowhere to be seen. *That was creepy*! He shivered and continued running up the street to his home.

When he arrived at his house, he wandered over to the side fence that separated his home from the new neighbor's house. They had moved in recently with a girl ten years old, just like him. *Hmmm, wonder if she's home.* At that moment, he heard arguing coming from inside the house.

As he peered over the fence, he saw a girl leaning against it. She had shoulder-length messy, blond hair.

Her face looked wet, and she kept wiping it with her hands over and over again. He realized she was crying.

"Hey! What's wrong?" he called over the fence.

She looked up in surprise. "Oh! You startled me. Didn't know anyone was around."

"Are you okay?"

She wiped her eyes with the back of her hand and smoothed her skirt. "I miss my friends and home."

Straightening up, she smiled weakly. "Sorry about this."

Mike felt awkward and decided

to change the subject.

"Saw your moving truck a few weeks ago. I'm Mike."

The girl looked relieved that the subject had changed. "I'm Mari. Nice to finally meet you."

"Hey, wanna go down to the park? There's an old tree there that I think you will find interesting."

"Interesting in what way?" She looked puzzled.

"I'll show you when we get to the park." Mike folded his arms to wait.

"Okay, got to tell my mom. Can you wait a minute?"

Mari smiled as she disappeared inside her home. Mike fiddled with some change in his pocket, glad to finally have something to do. She walked out of the gate wearing tan shorts, a T-shirt, and sandals.

Looking at her clothes, he thought, *that's better for playing down at the park.* "It's this way," he said, and the two began the short walk down to the park.

"Think you're going to like it here." Mike turned the corner from his sidewalk to the main street. "Almost always sunny and there are lots of friends to play with."

"Well, I guess." Mari frowned. "My dad says summer's the perfect time to move. Maybe it will be more peaceful here."

"Hmmm." Mike now remembered that he had found her crying, and felt uncomfortable, so he changed the subject. "What kind of sports do you like?"

"Oh, tennis, skiing, swimming, bike riding. How about you?"

Mike blurted out without a

thought, *"Football!* Yeah! Football's my favorite sport."

Mari smiled at his enthusiasm. "Oh, wait a minute. I forgot my drink. Got to go back and get it. Do you want one?"

"Sure. Meet you down there. The park's straight down this street at the end. You can't miss it."

"Okay." Mari ran up the hill.

Finally arriving at the park, Mike walked through the little playground nestled near the edge of a large grassy area.

Running through a few trees scattered around the perimeter, he stopped in front of the old tree to wait for his new friend. It was a small park so he couldn't miss her.

The memory of the glowing man came back into Mike's mind. Right then, Mari showed up.

"Okay, I'm finally ready."

"When I was down here earlier, this weird guy came up to me and tried to grab me." He shivered.

Mari turned full circle, taking in the entire park. "Well, is he still around? You're scaring me!"

Mike glanced behind him. "Don't see him." He grinned. "Let's forget about him. Come see the old tree I was telling you about."

"Okay, if you think it's safe."

"It's this way."

He shook off the memory of the glowing stranger and walked toward the tree, pointing at it.

Mari gasped. There it stood, with large, unusually vibrant green leaves that seemed to glow, and a trunk alive with energy. The old tree had the appearance of being from another world altogether.

"Wow!" She approached the old tree cautiously. "It's beautiful. Never seen anything like it."

"Been around a long time. My Dad told me it was almost cut down to make room for the elementary school."

"Looks like it belongs on another planet." Mari stared.

Putting his hand on the rough bark, Mike walked around the trunk, looking up into the branches high above him. Mari followed.

Dragging their hands along, they circled all the way around the old tree until they came back to their original position.

"Look how strong and old these branches are. This tree's so...*ohhh!*" She suddenly stepped back.

"What?" Then Mike watched the trunk opening up as if in slow motion until a gap stood before them big enough to allow someone to crawl inside.

"Yes!" he said with a grin.

Chapter Two

Inside the Old Tree

"Look at the trunk!" Mari leaned forward. "Bet someone could crawl right in."

"I've been inside before." Mike stared at the tree. "Let's go."

"Are there bugs and spiders in there?" Mari said timidly. "And what if the crack closes up on us?"

"Don't worry." Mike waved off her words. "Never closed up on me before. I've been inside at least four times. Come on."

Mari sighed. "Okay." She followed reluctantly, not willing to miss this adventure.

Watching as Mike dropped onto his knees and crawled through the opening, she followed cautiously, looking down around her hands for any bugs or spiders. *Oh, I don't like this.*

Standing up in the cool interior next to Mike, she found they were inside a spacious room with no bugs or crawling insects. She gazed around. *The inside looks bigger than the outside. How strange!*

Grass covered the entire floor

while tiny, delicate flowers of every color were planted around the edge. The walls were smooth and dry and softly lit by a source that filtered down from above her head.

She breathed in the wonderful scent of flowers, grass, and fresh dirt that permeated the space.

Mike looked at her. "Bet if we were with the right person, or said just the right thing, something exciting would happen!" He rubbed his arms, which had goose bumps all over them.

"Yeah, I feel the same way." Mari shivered.

Then the feeling faded and they were left sitting inside the strange tree. Mari started to feel shut in and turned to Mike. "That was weird! You ready to go?"

Mike grinned. "I like it in here."

"Come on. Let's go."

"Okay." He nodded, dropped onto his knees, and crawled out with Mari right behind him. As she moved through the opening into the bright sunlight, she squinted. Together, they watched the gap close in the trunk.

"You think the trunk will open up again?" She stood up outside the tree.

Mike thought for a moment and nodded. "Why not? It happened several times before. I discovered the old tree recently and wanted to share it with someone."

The sun was still high in the sky, and time seemed to have stood still while they were in the tree.

Mari thought she caught the glimpse of a dark shape moving behind another tree. But when she looked closer there was nothing there. *Just my imagination.* She shivered but didn't mention it to Mike, thankful to be heading out of the park.

"That was great. Only seen the tree do that a few times." Mike grinned.

"Sure was pretty inside. Did you see all the flowers?"

"Yeah, did you notice it looked bigger inside than out?"

"That was weird."

As they turned onto their street Mike asked, "Like to come swimming tomorrow?"

"I can't. I'll be visiting my grandparents. But thanks for showing me the old tree, Mike. Promise I won't tell anyone. See you when I get back."

They parted company outside his home, and he walked through the front door to the aroma of cooking coming from the kitchen. It smelled really good, but he could tell it wasn't pizza.

Maybe next time.

That night as Mike settled into bed, he gazed through his window, up into the night sky, with the full moon and stars shining down brightly, and thought of the strange tree and the even stranger glowing man. Something mysterious seemed to hover in the heavens.

He had a strong feeling he was on the verge of discovering a secret that lay deeply hidden. His world was not what it seemed to be—something more was waiting to be discovered.

He lay awake, thinking about his new friend, Mari, and the unusual tree they'd crawled into that afternoon. While listening to the night sounds outside, he fell asleep.

Chapter Three

Spot

Mike didn't see Mari for several days while she visited her grandparents. But the time flew by as he swam and went bike riding with his friends who had returned from camp and family vacations.

His dad also took him on several long bike rides and played video games with him, and they wrestled in the pool.

When he did see Mari again, she was sitting on her front porch with a guitar.

"Didn't know you could play." Mike said while sitting down next to her.

"Mom signed me up for guitar lessons. Says summer's a good time to learn something new." Mari strummed a few chords.

"Hmm, sounds okay, if you like the guitar."

"It's a little tricky, but I'm getting the hang of it." She played a simple tune for him, and it was pretty good.

"Always wanted to learn the drums," Mike volunteered. "But I'm still trying to convince my parents it won't be too loud." He jumped up onto the porch. "Hey, want to take a break and go to the park?"

"Okay, let's go see the old tree. Wonder if the trunk will open up again."

Mari put her guitar in the house and told her mom they were heading to the park. On the way, Mike noticed she appeared more comfortable and relaxed. *Must be getting used to living here.*

When they arrived, it was the hottest part of the day, so they had the park to themselves. Mike ran to the old tree with expectation and was excited when a small gap in the trunk opened and widened as he drew near.

He laughed. "Great! Been waiting for this."

Mari stepped back. "Can you go first?"

"No problem."

Dropping onto his hands and knees, he crawled through the gap and was surprised by what he found waiting inside. Instead of an empty interior with grass and dirt, a table covered with a red and white checkered tablecloth sat in the middle of the tree.

Mari's head appeared in the opening, and she stood up, shaking grass and dirt off her hands and knees. "Wow!" she gasped. "Look at all this." She pointed to the table.

Mike grinned. He noticed several chairs around the table with three place settings. On top of the red and white checkered table cloth was ice tea, lemonade, pizza, pretzels, licorice and every kind of dessert he could imagine, including ice cream.

A cute little gray and white dog appeared from behind a green curtain, a very similar color to the green of the tree. The curtain stood a little higher than Mike and Mari, dividing the inside of the tree in half.

"Oh, hello, young'uns!" said the dog, a playful smile on his face as his tail wagged. "I was told I'd have visitors today, so I set my table with the finest. My name is Spot. Come join me."

Mike and Mari looked at each other with expressions of disbelief.

"Hi," Mari said softly, staring at the dog. "I'm Mari."

"My names Mike and I'm confused." Mike spoke with more confidence than he felt inside. "Last time, this tree was empty. Now you're here? You're a dog, right?"

The animal chuckled. "I look like a dog, but then I might be something more, now mightn't I!"

Mike moved toward the dog. "Can you explain what you mean? I think I'm dreaming."

"You're not dreaming, Mike," Mari said to reassure him. "I'm seeing him too."

The small animal stood up on his hind legs, spread his paws out, and said, "Come and sit down young'uns. Let me explain things over some food."

Mike moved slowly toward the table, trying to figure out what was happening. Of course, dogs don't talk, and he needed to find a logical explanation for what he was seeing.

He sat down and glanced over at Mari. A look of wonder covered her face, and she smiled as the dog poured some lemonade into a tall glass filled with ice and handed it to her.

Mari sat back and relaxed, chatting with Spot as if she had conversation and lemonade with talking dogs every day. It took Mike longer to get comfortable, but the food helped. The food helped a lot.

The delicious meal consisted of pizza, pretzels, licorice, strawberries, apple pie, ice cream, and donuts that literally melted in your mouth. And there was this delicious, sweet, chocolate syrup that Mike poured over his ice cream, strawberries, and also succeeded in getting on his face and hands and even in his hair.

In fact, he managed to get more of the syrup on himself than on his meal. He was truly enjoying the feast in front of him.

The dog took a sip of lemonade. "Well now. I'm the guardian of this here tree. It leads to a wonderful place, and not just anybody's allowed inside. In fact, you two are special, or so I've been told. I'm gonna keep my eye on you. Think of me like a guardian *angel*." Spot winked at them and then laughed.

"I like you, my friends." Spot became excited and jumped off his chair. "Have you two met the prince, yet?"

"The who?" Mike asked.

"Why, the prince of the realm I'm guarding."

"A prince?" Mari said with surprise.

"Of course, young'un." Spot laughed and sat back down. "He's the nicest person you're ever gonna know and beautiful to look at, though not handsome in your world's terms; his kingdom doesn't go for that vanity stuff." He poured more lemonade into their glasses. "When the prince is around you feel safe, excited, and happy all rolled into one. And he's very powerful. Oh yes, he is very powerful indeed!"

"Oh!" exclaimed Mari. "It's like a fairytale, but this one is real?"

"Yes, indeedy, the prince's kingdom is even more real than yours. He loves your world and walks around in disguise as a humble worker among your people. Many of his subjects are with him in disguise, like me." Spot laughed. Then he asked seriously, "Are you interested in meeting him?"

Before Mike could stop her, Mari said, "Yes, he sounds great!"

"Wait a minute," Mike said slowly. "This is happening too fast. I'm just beginning to get used to you, and now you tell me about a prince. How do we know he's good?" Mike remembered the alarming stranger he'd met in the park earlier.

Spot looked offended and jumped off the chair, standing up on his hind legs. Pushing a paw into Mike's chest, he said, "Now look here. Don't you go talking bad about my prince and boss. There's nobody better than him and nobody kinder. Watch out 'cause he has a power no one else has. You've got to watch what you say! He's all good. There's no bad in him."

Mike leaned back in his chair and lifted his hands. "Okay, don't get upset."

Spot sat back down, looked at Mike for a minute, and then said, "You do know, don't you, that the minute you chose to come into this old tree you stepped over a threshold and out of time as you know it?"

Mike's eyes narrowed. "Wait. What?"

Spot leaned forward. "You're beginning to understand there's another world besides yours."

Mari smiled. "Another world besides ours? I like the sound of that." Her eyes shone.

Mike looked at his watch puzzled. "Mari, I really want to stay, but it should be getting late. My watch must have stopped. We need to get you home. Thanks for the food, Spot. We'll come back again."

"Well, I want you to know you can come visit me anytime." Spot smiled.

"Thanks." Mari patted the little dog's head. "Nice to meet you, and we will come see you again soon."

Mike shook Spot's paw and followed Mari out of the gap in the trunk. He looked up at the sun and around the park after he stood up.

"Weird, it doesn't look any later, but we were inside the tree for hours."

"Hmm, maybe time moves differently inside the tree," Mari suggested.

"Interesting thought." Mike nodded slowly.

They headed toward home in silence.

She stopped and looked at him. "What do you think about Spot and what he said?"

"Well, we both saw him, so he must be real. Who says there can't be another world alongside ours that we can't see? You can't see a black hole?"

Mari looked confused. "Black holes are in outer space, right? I've heard about them in school."

"Yeah, my dad says they are dark holes in space we can't see. Scientists believe they're there because of their influence on the stars, gas, and dust around them."

"I would like to meet the prince that Spot talked about." A puzzled expression came over Mari's face. "Why wasn't Spot there before?"

"Good question." Mike became quiet, and then his face lit up. "Maybe when people from Spot's world come into our world, sometimes you see them, and sometimes you can't."

Mari nodded and noticed they were at her home. "Hmmm, that sounds right." She moved up to her front door. "What a day, lots to think about. Bye."

Mike walked slowly to his front porch and paused for a moment with

29

his hand on the doorknob. He grinned. At the beginning of a boring summer, he had finally stumbled on an exciting adventure.

Chapter Four

Joshua

Early the next morning, Mike's friend Justin came over to swim. It was a hot day, but it flew by as they played in the refreshing water, squirting each other and roughhousing in the pool until his mother told them to settle down. Justin slept over, and that night Mike's mom gave them pizza and ice cream.

They stayed up late, and Mike almost told his friend about the old tree but decided Justin would think it was silly. It was now Mari's and his secret. Justin left early the next morning for basketball camp.

The days passed slowly. Then one morning, Mari came over bursting with news she had been waiting to tell Mike.

"Mike! I have to tell you" — Mari ran out of breath, took a deep gulp, and continued — "about what happened!"

"Calm down and start from the beginning." Mike took Mari outside to sit by the pool.

"Whew, let me catch my breath." As they dangled their feet in the water, she began again. "Okay, we had a man come to visit, and he stayed for dinner. He was really different."

"I'm thirsty, just a minute." Mike jumped up and headed into the house to get drinks. "Okay, go on." He gave one to Mari and she continued.

"Found out this man's known my dad for years and always shows up when things get bad. His name's Joshua." Mari told Mike how her father had met Joshua as a child. Recently, he had appeared again. "Supposed to be really old, but he looks young and is a master carpenter. Saw some of his furniture. It's amazing."

Mike tried to follow Mari's conversation. "This is confusing."

"I know. I don't understand the

age thing. But Joshua wants to take us to a special park this afternoon. I told him to come here so you could join us." Mari visibly relaxed. "You want to go, Mike?"

"Sure, but our park with the old tree is pretty special," He reminded her.

They'd gone to the kitchen to refill their drinks when the doorbell rang. When they opened the door, standing on the porch was a man of average height with brown hair, smiling at them. Mike immediately liked him.

Mari introduced him as Joshua. He asked to speak with Mike's mom, who was upstairs attempting to write a children's book on her computer.

When she came down, they discussed where they would be going and when they would be back. Mike was surprised to hear that they were heading to the park.

As they were walking out of his house, Mari whispered. "Do you think we should tell him about the old tree?"

"No, it's our secret."

"But he's taking us to the park. I think we can trust him. You tell him, Mike," pleaded Mari under her breath.

"You do it," Mike whispered back.

"Okay," she said reluctantly. "Ah, Joshua, we have s-something to tell you. This park has an unusual tree in it."

"Yes, I know." Joshua smiled. "A very old tree."

"But what you don't know is"— Mari looked at Mike for support—"a gap appeared big enough to crawl through."

"Go on." Joshua had a twinkle in

his eye and looked as though he was about to laugh.

Mike joined in with embarrassment. "Now don't laugh, but when we went inside, there was a talking dog—sounds crazy—oh, and a table with pizza, lemonade, and this amazing chocolate syrup."

Joshua laughed. "Sounds right. You met my friend, Spot."

"How'd you know that?" Mari said with surprise.

"He told me all about it." Joshua looked deep into their eyes. "Your world is not what it appears to be."

What a funny thing to say, Mike thought. It reminded him of what their new friend Spot had said, and it made Mike wonder.

When he looked into Joshua's eyes, Mike noticed they were the kindest he had ever seen.

The group arrived at the park and Joshua walked up to the old tree and turned, motioning them to follow. Then he walked through the trunk and vanished.

"Did you see that? It looked like he went right through the tree trunk?" Mike said with wonder.

Mari was speechless.

Mike walked right up to the trunk and pushed his hand against it. It was definitely solid. He dropped on both knees and led the way through the gap. When they both stood up inside, Joshua was waiting for them, but Spot was nowhere to be found.

The table, chairs, and the feast were missing, but the floral scent of grass and fresh flowers permeated the space. Soft light filtered down onto the sides of the tree and lit up the tiny flowers around the edge of the interior.

Suddenly, a door opened on the other side of the trunk. Joshua looked at them and said, "Take my hands and trust me."

Mike remembered the feeling he'd had the first time they'd crawled into the tree: if they were with the right person or said just the right thing, a great adventure would open up for them. They were with the right person now!

As he went through the door, Mike expected to walk out into the park. Instead, he stood in the back of a huge room that appeared to have no ceiling.

When he looked down at his feet, a golden floor glittered up at him.

It was filled with thousands and thousands of people, animals, birds, and other unusual creatures standing together, facing forward.

He glanced over at Mari, whose face was shining with wonder. He could feel the excitement welling up inside him and tried to calm down.

Joshua led them up the center of the enormous room, and the crowd, on each side, turned to watch as they walked past. Mike looked into their faces, and they smiled back at him even though they stood in silence.

It was so quiet he could hear his feet shuffling on the shiny floor, which looked very much like gold. A brilliant amber light filled the room, but the source of it was confusing as it came from everywhere at once. The golden floor and sheer size of the room along with the enormous crowd standing quietly gave him the feeling this place had been created for royalty.

Mike took Mari's hand, and together they continued up the aisle toward the front of the gigantic room. It seemed to take a long time, but at last they reached the steps leading up to an exquisite throne where a king sat.

A crystal, blue expanse in front of the throne reminded Mike of water, and he held his breath as they drew near the steps. The way the brilliant light reflected around him made it hard to see clearly. The great king sitting on the throne seemed to be the source of much of that light.

The small group finally arrived at the bottom of the steps leading up to the throne. Joshua went up and sat down on the throne, next to the king. Mari was trembling, and Mike couldn't figure out what to do with his hands. But they both knew without a doubt that they were now in the presence of a great and powerful person.

Joshua leaned close to the king,

giving him a big hug. He was not in the least bit intimidated or afraid of the king, but happy and joyful to be with him.

Now the king turned and focused on Mike and Mari. Mike became very quiet and was filled with awe. He looked over at Mari, watching her clasp and unclasp her hands nervously.

When the king spoke, his musical voice sounded like a waterfall. "Welcome, Mike and Mari, I have been waiting for you. I knew you would be coming to help."

Mike decided the king had mistaken them for someone else, but his thoughts were interrupted when he spoke again.

"I have a gift for each of you."

Mike's ears perked up when he heard the word *gift*. *Maybe this king knows what he's talking about.*

The ruler continued, "You have been brought here to receive training for a great battle if you agreed to stay and help. An evil creature from this kingdom is now on your world and has already caused a great deal of sorrow."

Mike looked over at Mari and saw the shock on her face.

The king went on. "This evil creature has brought chaos into almost every area of life in your world."

Mike & Mari felt a loving presence enveloping them as the king spoke.

"Your friend Joshua is actually my only son, who travels between worlds and has been warring with the evil being for a long time."

"Many faithful subjects from our realm are in your world in a hidden form, and some of the people from your world already have joined forces with them in their battle against the evil being."

Mike sensed that this king was very loving, good, and kind. He radiated warmth but also an authority and power that Mike had never sensed before.

He felt excited to be asked to join this struggle but wondered how Mari would feel about being trained for a great battle.

At that point Joshua got up from his father's side and walked down the steps. He took Mike's and Mari's hands and led them out of the throne room and into an armory. There he introduced them to Herald.

Herald was the person (if you could call him that) who was to train Mike and Mari in the art of warfare.

A tall birdlike creature, he reminded Mike of an eagle but larger. His pale yellow, probing eyes enabled him to see for long distances, which, he explained, made him valuable in battle.

"This realm is at war with someone who is full of hatred and rage toward Joshua, the king and your world. He was once part of our kingdom but chose evil instead of good." Herald's large eyes studied Mike.

"You see," he said. "Joshua, along with those of his kingdom, have entered your world to fight this evil that has defiled it. They are your guardians, children, and want to protect your people."

"Do you know a dog named Spot?" Mari asked.

"Why do you ask?" Herald turned his piercing eyes on her.

"We met him in an old tree."

"Spot's one of us." Herald nodded his beaked head. "He is one of the guardians of your world."

"He spoke of a prince." Mike volunteered.

"The prince he spoke of is Joshua. He chooses to appear in your world as a humble, simple man but, as you can see, he is the king's only son." Herald turned and picked up two swords. "Now we must begin your training so you can fight along with us in the great battle."

He handed one sword to Mike and the other to Mari, and the next few hours were extremely exciting. Mike was allowed to do things he could never had done at home and was given permission to fight and play with a very sharp object, in this case, an real sword. He found this exhilarating and could have gone on practicing for a very long time.

Mike had noticed that time was different inside the tree then outside in his park. He wondered how much time if any would pass at home before they finished their training here.

Herald also gave him his very own set of armor and a beautiful shield with a tree painted on it that looked very much like the old tree in the park. Unusual creatures helped teach and train him; some appeared to be birds while others looked like men. Even what appeared to be dogs and lions dropped in to help teach and train.

Mike stood back to watch Mari. She was enjoying the sword play, and becoming skilled at handling the shield as well.

He resumed his training with Herald and was exceptionally quick with the sword as he lunged at his instructor. Proud of Mike's skill and progress, Herald began teaching him advanced moves. "You learn quickly, my son. Try this." Herald showed him an especially difficult move, which Mike mastered with ease.

Mike and Mari glanced over at each other from time to time, as if to ask, *is this real?* They were having the time of their lives.

After they had practiced for a long time, Joshua approached and asked if they would join him for supper. He led them into a beautiful pavilion of every color of the rainbow, and they sat around a huge, intricately carved wooden table with people and creatures dressed in the most magnificent clothing.

Mari particularly enjoyed the robes and jewels. "Mike, look. Have you ever see so many jewels on one person?"

"Who cares about jewels? Look at that armor. Never seen anything like it." Mike pointed to a knight sitting across the table from him. The pieces looked silver but could easily have been white gold, and many sparkling jewels were set in the armor in intricate designs.

The children sat next to a badger who looked like a knight. He stood and bowed gracefully when introduced.

"Do you know a dog named Spot?" Mike thought if Herald the eagle knew Spot then he might as well.

The badger spoke with a twinkle in his eyes. "Why, of course. One of our finest. He's actually a good friend of mine. When he isn't guarding the old tree we plan battle strategies together. Great chap, you know."

Chap. Now that was a strange word, and Mike pictured these two having tea and scones together.

"We met him inside the old tree the other day. He gave us pizza and all kinds of treats. My favorite was the chocolate syrup." Mike fingered his hair and then looked around, hoping to find it on this table as well.

"Ah yes, we heard about your meeting. Very strategic. Yes, very strategic." The badger started humming, and his eyes had a far-off look in them.

They redirected their attention to Herald as he began a speech about Joshua and the king. Excitement filled the air, and they were party to many toasts to Joshua, his father, Mike, and Mari. This went on for quite a while, and just as Mike was growing tired and becoming really hungry, Joshua turned to him with a smile. "And now, my knight, it's time to eat."

"Your knight? I like the sound of that." The adventure was already working a change in Mike.

"My father and I want to give those in your world the freedom to come out from under the enemy's rule."

Mike frowned. "I never knew about this enemy." He remembered the glowing stranger he'd met in the park. "There was a glowing man that was asking questions about the tree and tried to grab me. Is he the enemy that you are talking about?"

"Yes, Mike, many don't know about him, but we fight to free them."

Joshua put a hand on Mike's shoulder and then left to talk to his other subjects. Mike watched as he hugged, patted, and spoke to each one.

His deep love for his friends was apparent as the prince paused to talk to each of them. They responded to him with love and loyalty.

The badger blinked as if awakening from a dream, turned, and said to Mari and Mike, "Well, what do you think of your adventure so far?"

"It's fun." Mike pointed down. "Really like the sword and armor."

The badger nodded. "It looks fine on you, young man, very fine indeed. Why, you look like a true warrior of the realm."

At last, the food arrived and Mike tore into it. After dinner, he moved on to the many desserts available. Looking around, he spied what appeared to be the chocolate syrup he had so loved while having pizza with Spot.

"Hey! Can someone pass me that

silver bowl?" Mike pointed. His neighbor handed it to him.

When the bowl arrived, he was delighted to see that it was indeed the syrup Spot had offered them in the old tree. It must be served only in this realm because he had never tasted anything like it before.

Pouring it over everything on his plate, he got down to the task of eating. At last, knowing he could not swallow another bite, he sat back to rest for a minute, listening to the conversation going on around him.

He felt disappointed when Joshua came over and told him it was time to go. "We need to get you and Mari back home."

"Do we have to go?" Mike pleaded. "I want to stay longer."

"Yes, Mike. But you will return at the same time you left. Time stands still in your world while you are inside the old tree and go through it to other lands." Joshua put his hand on Mike's shoulder. "Don't worry. There will be many more adventures."

As they walked toward the tree entrance, Joshua asked Mari how she was doing at home.

She made a funny face that looked like she might cry, and stared at her feet.

Joshua said softly. "Mari, every-thing will work out. Give it time. I'm here to help you and your parents. Trust me!"

Mike headed out into the park while Joshua sat with Mari inside the tree for a few minutes. He was glad to see Joshua talking with her. When she walked out, she seemed more peaceful, and the pain had left her face.

He walked them back to Mike's

mom, and they all sat in the living room, chatting for a few minutes. Then Joshua left.

Mike moved onto the front porch and turned to Mari. "Do you want to come over tomorrow, we could go swimming?"

Her face lit up then she frowned. "Oh, I can't. The family's going to a marriage counselor. Then we're spending the rest of the day together."

"What's a marriage counselor?"

Mari was quiet for a minute. "It's a person trained to help those in a marriage that isn't working. The counselor wants the whole family there to talk to us."

"Doesn't sound like much fun." Mike blurted out.

"I know but I don't have a choice. Bye."

As Mike closed the front door he

thought, *whew, what a day!*

Chapter Five

Evil in the Throne Room

Mike was busy with family the next few days.

Then one morning, he awoke to a knock on the door. Mari was waiting for him.

"Gotta show you something," she said excitedly.

"Come in. I'll be back in a minute." Mike ran up the stairs.

When he came back down, she grabbed his hand and took him over to a big mirror in the family room.

"Look, see the armor we received during our training in Joshua's kingdom?"

He studied his reflection in the mirror. "Whoa, it's supposed to be invisible here. It disappeared when we came home."

Mari admired her armor in the reflection. "But look. It's visible."

"Guess it's only visible when we're looking in the mirror." Mike glanced over at Mari and then pointed at her. "Look. I'm beginning to see your armor without the mirror, but it's really faint."

When they talked about Joshua and his kingdom, the armor would grow more solid and less hazy.

She looked at him and giggled. "Now I can see yours too. Isn't this fun?"

"See how the light bounces off us and fills the room?" Mike looked around in surprise.

"Yeah, and look at the armor. It's almost solid."

Mike's mom called down from upstairs, asking if everything was all right. Before they could answer, she came down to check on them.

He held his breath as his mom walked into the room, wondering how she would react to their strange armor and the light that reflected off it. She talked to them normally and then went back upstairs.

After she left, Mari turned to

Mike. "She didn't see any of this."

"Yeah, I guess other people can't see the armor." Mike stood admiring himself in the mirror again. "Maybe we shouldn't tell anyone about this yet."

"Why?" Mari looked at Mike with a puzzled expression on her face.

"I think we should keep it between us, for now."

"Still don't see why."

"Let's just keep it quiet and see what happens next," Mike said.

Mari looked hurt and shook her head. "Aren't we getting a little bossy. It's my decision who I tell!"

"I didn't mean to be bossy. Just want to wait to tell people."

Mari visibly relaxed and then nodded. "Okay, but at some point, I'm sharing it. We may find we're not the only ones having these adventures."

"Okay, now that we agree on

that, let's go to the old tree." Mike headed for the front door and grabbed his football on the way out. "Hope Joshua's down there."

"Me too!" Mari held out her hands to catch the ball.

Suddenly Mike had a thought. "Remember the king told us the evil creature came here from his realm? Joshua said the evil creature was the glowing man that tried to grab me at the park, in front of the tree."

"Oh really?" Mari thought for a minute. "And Joshua also said that others from our world had been trained just like us."

Mike blurted out. "Maybe we can see their armor too."

Mari nodded in agreement.

Mike focused back on his armor and studied the sword as well. The gold handle was engraved with creatures he had seen in the throne room: winged beings and majestic people dressed for war were on the hilt.

As he looked more closely, he saw words engraved onto the blade shift into sentences about love and kindness, life and death, and war and peace. He also found writing there that he didn't understand.

Remembering the football in his other arm, he tossed it to Mari, who caught it and then threw it back with skill.

"Hey, where'd you learn to throw like that?" Mike asked.

"From older brothers."

"Aren't you an only child?"

"No, I used to hang out with them and their friends."

Mike asked, "Where are your older brothers now?"

"One of my brothers is in college, and the other two moved out a while ago."

They arrived at the park, and there was Joshua leaning against the old tree, waiting for them. They both ran up, and Mari hugged him.

"Look at our armor?" Mike pointed to Mari and himself.

Joshua smiled. "I wondered when you'd discover that."

"Do others from our world have this armor too?" Mari looked into Joshua's kind eyes.

"Yes, they do."

Mike interrupted. "Are we going through the old tree again?"

"That's why I'm here. Follow me." He walked right through the trunk and disappeared. Mike walked right into the trunk and bounced off, falling to the ground.

Mari put her hand over her mouth to stifle a laugh. "Think we still need to go in the old way."

They both dropped onto their knees and crawled into the tree. This time, their friend Spot was waiting for them inside.

"Howdy, y'all." He bowed to Joshua. "It's an honor to have you here, sire."

"Spot, good to see you. Give me a hug." Joshua extended his arms out, and Spot bounded up to him, put his paws on the prince's shoulders, and gave him a big lick on the face. "That's better, my friend." Joshua said with a laugh.

They waved goodbye to Spot as Joshua led them through the door on the other side of the tree and into the huge room. Mike walked slowly up the golden path that led to the king and stopped at the steps by the foot of the throne. Joshua walked up and sat down next to his father.

To Mike's surprise, Joshua then motioned for them to come up and join him. Mari and Mike looked at each other, and both beamed with delight. Holding hands, they walked up the steps and into the light.

Joshua pointed toward a seat on his right side. Mike sat down next to him, silenced by the shock of where he was sitting. Mari sat down next to him.

The room vibrated with power. Occasionally, Mike heard the sound of thunder and then a flash of lightning struck different places in the room. Yet he had never felt so much peace, safety, and love as he sat back and took in the atmosphere. After a while, Joshua stood up and took their hands, leading them to a side chamber.

As they walked to the room, Mike stopped in the entrance and stared, the doors looked like they were made of pearl. Everything in the room was draped in soft silk, satin, or some other exquisite cloth, and jewels were embedded in the walls and ceiling. Mari stood for a long time gazing upward, and Mike decided she was having a hard time tearing her eyes away from the sparkling jewels.

The sofas were made of an elegant, soft, luscious material, and the rug was deep and thick. The colors in the room were rich and calming. Mike relaxed as a deep peace and rest filled his soul. He had never been in a room like this, and a royal chamber on Mike's world would have appeared as a cheap copy.

Joshua motioned them farther into the room. "This is a place for you to rest. There are couches to sleep on and refreshments as well."

Looking around, Mike noticed several kinds of creatures in the room with him. The first group were very tall, twice his height, and dressed in magnificent gold armor with swords at their sides. They had human features and reminded Mike of mighty warriors.

The second group consisted of little round creatures strumming small instruments and singing softly. They looked like soft, round children, but their faces were those of someone wise and timeless. These were dressed in beautiful, flowing robes of the deepest, richest colors and from time to time floated through the room in a flying dance.

Mari sat back on a deep, soft blue couch. "Isn't that music beautiful?"

Mike nodded and plopped down on another deep blue couch close to Mari, putting his feet up and his hands behind his head.

A third group of creatures came into view that were hard to describe. They looked like balls of light with a man standing inside holding a sword, and rotating so fast he appeared to be facing every direction at once.

As Mike sat back on the soft sofa, he heard a commotion in the great hall, and a stir went through the creatures in the room. Joshua turned toward them with his finger on his lips. "Listen now and you will learn something important."

Mike could now hear someone speaking very loudly and arrogantly to the king on the throne. The words were muffled inside the room, but he strained to hear what was being said.

"What's going on?" Mike felt anxious.

"Yeah, what's happening?" Mari had a worried look on her face.

"It's the evil creature we told you about. Don't worry. Everything's going to be all right." Joshua smiled at them and left the room to join his father.

Suddenly, it became very quiet, and Mike could hear the creature clearly. "Oh, Majestic One!" It sounded like he snickered. "You have two of my own within your chamber, and you must give them back to me. They do not deserve to be here in this beautiful realm, and you know this very well."

Mike heard a deep rumbling, fierce and powerful and then the king's voice. "Oh, enemy of all things living and all that is good, be it known to you that they are accompanied here by my son, so you have no claim on them, nor

69

can you touch them."

The evil creature answered with a voice that sounded very persuasive and logical. "But, so-called king of kings, let me tell you all the bad things they have done and thought and all the good things they have withheld from those around them. I have listed every-thing here on this scroll."

To his horror, Mike realized the evil creature was talking about them, and he blushed as he listened to the scroll being read. *He sure keeps a good record*, thought Mike, *and he doesn't miss a thing!*

As the evil creature droned on and on about their misdeeds, a tall, armored creature came over and offered Mike grapes, strawberries and something that looked similar to lemonade.

"Welcome, my name is Mie. I am

an arc." He handed Mike a drink. "Let me know if you need anything else. You can rest here."

"What will happen to us?" Mari's voice quavered as she looked up at the tall arc.

"Do not fear. Prince Joshua and his father will take care of everything." Mie bowed to Mari as he spoke.

She opened the door and peeked out. Mike stepped behind her and saw the evil creature. It looked like one of the arcs, tall and stately—almost beautiful, but in a terrifying way. He realized it was the glowing stranger who had talked to him in front of the tree and tried to grab him. He wanted to close the door, but the evil creature turned and looked straight into his eyes.

Mike froze in the doorway, unable to move. His mind was full of fear and panic, and he desperately wanted to tear his eyes away from the creature; but he was strangely drawn to those eyes so beautiful but so cold and cruel. He shuddered, and then he thought of Joshua and his father, and he looked over at them. The spell was instantly broken, and now Mike was able to turn and close the door.

While the door had been open, all the creatures in the room had stood perfectly still, waiting to see what Mike would do. When he turned his mind away from the evil creature and put it on Joshua and his father, they all broke into singing and dancing, and the room was full of joy.

Mie, the arc who had originally spoken to Mike, approached again. "You resisted! You were wise, Mike, to turn your thoughts from the evil one. His name is Sitnaw, and he is an arc, just like I am. We are a race of warrior beings created by the king and Joshua, but Sitnaw was thrown out of our kingdom. He now uses fear and terror to control your world. You chose to put your mind on the prince and his father. This is what saved you."

Mike looked up with relief. "Whew, that was close. Thought the creature had me for a minute."

The arc put his hand on Mike's shoulder. "To my shame, I used to look up to the greatness of that evil one, for there was no other like him in this realm. He also thought himself great and became prideful."

Mie offered Mike and Mari something that looked like chocolate chip cookies. "For a long time, he served the king faithfully, but after a while, he grew rebellious and wanted to replace the king and sit on the

73

throne to be worshipped."

Mie continued, looking very sad. "The evil creature had a violent fight with the king and convinced other arcs to join him in waging war against the king and his son."

He sighed. "And a terrible battle raged until Sitnaw and his arcs were thrown out of the kingdom."

"Whoa! That's who's out there now?" Mike felt shock and fear.

"Yes. He persuaded many in our realm to follow him, convincing them that they did not have to obey the king anymore. The time is coming when Sitnaw and his minions will be judged severely but not yet. They are powerful and will do you great harm unless you remain under the protection of the king and his son."

At that moment, to everyone's relief, Joshua came back into the room.

He had Mike and Mari sit down next to him on a big, comfortable sofa. With a smile, he hugged both of them and then turned to Mike.

"Well done, my son. The evil creature has no control over your mind if you turn it from his fear tactics and put it on my father and me. Thoughts of us will always fill you with hope, peace, and rest."

Mike nodded seriously, having just learned an important lesson. "I met him earlier near the old tree." He frowned.

"Sitnaw roams freely in your world. We fight to release your people from his evil." Joshua told Mari and Mike that this was why he had brought them here, and now it was time to head back to the other world.

Walking to the door leading into the great hall, Joshua opened it. Mike held his breath, but to his relief, the evil creature was nowhere to be seen. He and Mari said goodbye to the king, hugged and thanked him, and then walked back through the great hall.

At the back of the enormous room, instead of going through the door that led into the old tree, Joshua took them to his city for a short peek. He led them outside under a perfectly blue sky and a bright, golden sun.

Stretched out before Mike lay a magnificent city with huge towers and castles as far as he could see, with their flags flying in the wind. Everywhere he looked, he was surrounded by rolling, green hills dotted with magnificent trees and colorful flowers. A butterfly came and landed on Mari's hand. It was beautiful to look at with unusual colors that Mike didn't recognize, shimmering from its wings.

Joshua's world was richer and more beautiful than Mike and Mari's world. This seemed to be the real thing and theirs a mere copy.

Mari sighed. "I'd like to stay here for a long time."

Joshua studied her for a minute. "This is truly a wonderful place, but it's time to go back now. Don't worry. We'll visit here again."

He led them into the great hall again and through the door that led to the old tree. When they stepped inside, Spot greeted them.

"Hi there, young'uns. How's about some tea?"

"Thank you, Spot, but we can't right now. I need to get Mike and Mari back to their families." Joshua gave his friend a big hug. Taking Mike and Mari's hands, he walked them right through the wall of the tree.

Leading them through the park, he gave each a big hug, and then said goodbye. Mike led the way home while Mari talked excitedly about all they had seen.

Chapter Six

Camping

A few days later, Mike waved goodbye to Mari and his other friends as he headed out for the summer camping trip with his parents. He'd been looking forward to this trip for a long time.

The car was crammed with camping gear and sleeping bags. After several hours of driving, Mike found himself heading down a highway surrounded by endless desert, and he watched the beautiful scenery pass by outside his car window.

First, the highway went through large sand dunes, and then the land-scape changed to huge rock formations filling his view in every direction. He imagined the rocks were giants playing games with each other or taking naps.

"This desert's too dead to have anything living in it." Mike waited for a reply.

"Things aren't always as they appear." His dad continued. "Even though it looks barren and dead, the desert's full of all kinds of plant, animal, and insect life."

Mike peered out the window. "Don't see any. Well, maybe a few bushes."

His dad took a sip of water. "The animals and insects are small and live underground. Larger animals such as coyotes and owls come out at night and hunt for food."

Now Mike looked more closely, hoping to get a glimpse of the animals his dad had just described. He noticed trees with branches lifted upward to the sky and little flowers growing on them.

"Hey, Dad, what are those?"

"They're called Joshua trees and a good example of what grows out here."

Finally, they drove up to the campsite. Jumping out of the car, Mike began to explore, while his mom set up the camp stove and his dad dragged their tent out of the trunk.

"Mike, come here and help me with this," his dad yelled.

"Do I have to? I want to explore."

"I need your help. Plenty of time to explore later.

"Come on. Let me look around."

"Not now. Please come and help me."

Mike's shoulders slumped in disappointment as he looked out over the rocky wilderness that stretched out in all directions. Dragging himself over to his dad, he started helping him set up the tents.

He felt his dad's hand on his shoulder. "Thanks, buddy. You did a great job. Now we can go explore together." Suddenly, Mike had a burst of energy and raced over to a large rock formation near a Joshua tree.

It was starting to get dark when they returned to camp, and Mike flopped down next to a roaring fire. As he glanced around the campsite, he saw a table set with a feast for a king, and his empty stomach growled. He realized it had been a long time since lunch.

After dinner, Mike sat back, listening to his dad's campfire songs, and before long, his eyes were closed. When the music stopped, he sleepily headed for the tent, changed into his pajamas, and shivered in the cold. It didn't take long to warm up in the sleeping bag, and he fell fast asleep listening to the crackle of the fire and his parents talking softly.

In the middle of the night, he woke up to the sound of coyotes howling in the distance. They came closer and closer, yelping with an eerie high pitch, as if the pack had found food. He shivered.

Turning over in his sleeping bag, he was startled to see Joshua's head inside the tent, and his finger over his lips. Joshua motioned him to come outside.

As Mike emerged from the tent, Joshua said, "I'm here to protect you. The coyotes approaching aren't what they appear to be, but part of the evil that's entered your world."

"Hmmm." Mike looked into the tent to check on his parents. They were sleeping soundly.

"Don't worry. Your parents will be asleep throughout the night. You ready?"

"Yeah." Mike nodded.

Joshua motioned him to wait a minute. "Remember the evil creature you saw in the throne room?"

"I'll never forget." Mike said. "Same man I met at the old tree."

"That's right. I told you his name is Sitnaw, and he now roams your world for a time releasing destruction and evil. But there is a time coming when he will be judged."

Mike shivered. "What can I do? How can I help?"

"As I teach you how to use my authority, you will be able to do many things in my name. First, these coyotes can't be defeated by human will or strength. They serve Sitnaw." Joshua pointed to Mike's clothing.

Looking down, Mike could no longer see his flannel pajamas. His armor had become completely solid. Pulling out his sword, he saw words engraved on it shining bright red like blood, "All things are under His feet."

Mike's shield glowed with the white light he'd seen in the throne room shining off the king. Looking over at Joshua, he was startled to see Joshua in brilliant, white armor, his hair shining pure white and his skin glowing with a golden light.

"I am with you, Mike. Don't be afraid. Always call on me when the enemy comes against you." He placed his hand on Mike's shoulder. "I've already defeated him in my realm, but you and the inhabitants of this planet must join me and my people and defeat him here. It's a matter of choice. That's the key—choice. Each person must choose who he will serve. And now it's time to fight!"

"I'm ready!"

To Mike's amazement, he and Joshua suddenly lifted off the ground and began to fly like eagles above the campground. He could see everything in the dark, and he decided it had something to do with Joshua. Far below, they saw a black, swarming pack of coyotes working its way down a hill toward the campground. As Mike looked off to the right, he noticed an old man on a bike riding down a small path. *That's strange.*

Joshua pointed to the hunched figure of the old man. "Look! It's Sitnaw, transformed into another shape. We must prevent him from meeting up with the coyotes."

They dove down, down, down with a speed that Mike had never experienced before. It was breathtaking and exhilarating to be traveling that fast. The cold night air whipped against Mike's face, and the night sounds rose up to meet them as they came down and landed right behind the old man on the bike.

"He can't see us," Joshua said. "Don't be afraid. My father is watching over us. Now pay attention."

He drew out a golden net and flung it over the old man who turned into the evil creature, Sitnaw. Suddenly, two huge arcs appeared on each side of Sitnaw and tied a knot in the net.

Turning to Joshua, they said in unison, "We will take him back to the king." Instantly, they disappeared with the evil creature.

Mike turned in a circle. "Where'd they go?"

"Back to my realm to appear before my father. You've done well tonight, Mike."

"But I didn't do anything."

"There, you are mistaken. You were willing to spend time with me tonight, which allowed this evil to be caught and bound. Do not underestimate your times with me, my son. They are precious and powerful."

Mike looked at Joshua in the moonlight. "Think I understand. But what happened to the coyotes?"

Joshua ruffled Mike's hair. "They disbanded and hid when they saw we'd defeated their leader."

"Thanks for protecting me and my parents."

"I'm always with you. Call me anytime, day or night."

Joshua and Mike flew back to the campsite and landed on the ground beside the tent. Mike peeked in to see his parents sleeping soundly. His armor began to fade, and he could see his pajamas reappearing again. Unexpectedly, Joshua disappeared, and Mike was left standing in the tent in silence.

He burrowed down into the sleeping bag, thinking about Joshua and the coyotes. Finally, sleep overtook him, and he fell into a deep slumber.

Chapter Seven

The Battle at Sea

To Mike's relief, the rest of the camping trip continued as normal. He saw beautiful sights, walked along nature trails, and enjoyed the music and company around the campfire. Soon it was time to pack up the car and head back down the road through the desert toward home.

When Mike drove onto his street, Mari was waiting for him. He waved at her as their car pulled into his driveway and jumped out.

"Guess what?" His face was flushed with excitement.

"What?" She walked over to him.

"Joshua showed up."

"Really?"

"Yeah, and I saw that scary guy Sitnaw again. Joshua and I stopped him from doing more bad things."

Mike told the details of the adventure, and Mari sat quietly listening with amazement on her face.

They decided to walk down to the park and see what was going on at the old tree. When they arrived, a large gap was already opening in the trunk. Mari followed Mike through the opening. He stood up in the cool interior and found Joshua and Spot sitting at the red and white checkered table, drinking ice tea.

"Hi, Mike. Hi, Mari! We've been expecting you." Joshua pointed to two chairs next to him at the table. "Come sit down and join us."

"We were hoping you'd be here." Mike grabbed a chair next to Joshua.

When they were all seated, Joshua began, "This is a very special day. We will not be going through the old tree but staying on your world today. Many from your world and from my realm are gathering down by the ocean. There will be a great battle between good and evil this day."

Joshua spoke calmly but Mike

sensed sadness in his voice as he continued. "Don't be afraid. I will defeat Sitnaw and dismantle his evil power over your planet. You will also be in this battle, using the weapons given you by my father."

Mike felt excitement well up inside. "Wow, we actually get to fight with the swords Herald gave us?"

"Aren't you scared, Mike?" Mari said in a small voice.

"Not really. Joshua has this."

Joshua nodded. "Don't be afraid. Even though all of this will be hidden from the people in your world, you will have the ability to see all the creatures in the battle, good and evil. Remember: don't be frightened. Good will triumph over evil."

Joshua got up and led them out of the tree, through their park and down a road toward the ocean. It was a peaceful day, and the sun shone down while a gentle breeze brought the smell of the sea onto the path. Mike could see the beach ahead as the trail opened up, and the golden ocean sparkled in front of him, with the sun's rays reflecting off it.

A countless numbers of strange-looking animals and people were gathered, clustered in small groups all over the beach, dressed in full armor with swords and shields hanging by their sides.

When Joshua approached the throng, there was a hush as everyone turned toward him, awaiting orders. Mike and Mari noticed that their own armor had become solid again.

As he looked out to sea, Mike watched a dark, menacing presence descend onto the water. Ancient ships floating on the ocean surface began to battle with one another. These ships reminded him of ones he had seen in books during history class.

Joshua reached out and took their hands. "Get ready. Don't worry about what's going to happen. When you're with me, anything's possible!"

Before Mike knew it, Joshua had stepped out onto the water holding both of their hands. Looking around in disbelief, he watched Joshua walk on top of the waves! As Mike walked beside Joshua, he looked down and realized he too was standing on the waves, not sinking down under them. This was getting more exciting every minute.

The three of them simply walked out, on top of the water, to where the ships were battling each other. This was a dangerous time for them because the war had started in earnest, and they were moving right into the line of fire. But he had faith in Joshua and knew he would protect them.

Mike now counted a dozen ancient-looking ships on each side. Smoke from numerous fires made his eyes water. Periodically, he heard a loud boom and then something flew by him and exploded on one of the decks, sending those onboard scrambling. Joshua had both Mike and Mari duck several times, as objects whizzed over their heads, barely missing them. Now Mike felt afraid, but there was also a strange, new strength and daring mingled with excitement moving him forward.

Finally, they managed to climb onto one of the ships. It was flying a banner with a tree emblem on it—a tree that looked exactly like the old tree in the park. Mike looked around the ship and immediately recognized Spot. He ran over with Mari.

"Oh, Spot, you're here too!" Mari gave him a big hug.

"Do you think I'd miss this, young'un?"

"Good to see you again, Spot. Proud to be fighting next to you." Mike patted him on the shoulder.

"It's an exciting day. This is the day we strip the evil one of his power. This'll help many in your world be able to accept what the prince offers them. And many will choose him, my friend. Many will!"

"Hello there." Up walked Herald, the eagle who had trained the children. "Didn't I tell you there'd be a great battle and we would fight in it?"

"Thanks for all the training, Herald." Mike bowed. "Now we'll get a chance to fight."

Herald nodded approvingly and smiled. "I think, my son, this will be more a battle of will and thought than actual sword play. Use your sword and shield, but also remember to fight off the thoughts the enemy sends your way."

"What kind of thoughts?"

"Discouragement, despair, and hopelessness are some of his tactics. If you're not alert, you'll think they're your own feelings and thoughts. Remember—keep alert."

Mike looked across to another vessel flying a flag with the old tree emblem, and he recognized the badger they'd sat with at dinner in Joshua's kingdom. The badger was very busy working with the creatures on his ship. The enemy had succeeded in throwing a net onto the badger's ship, and many had become entangled in it.

"Joshua, come quickly." Mike pointed.

Joshua came up beside Mike. "Looks like his ship is removed from battle for the moment."

Other vessels flying the old tree emblem were having trouble as well. They were throwing their swords down and diving off the sides of the ship into the freezing water below. Mike could hear chilling jeers and howls coming from the enemy's ships surrounding them. The battle was not going well.

Cruel weapons were used by Sitnaw. They filled Mike with terror as he watched helplessly. He turned his head away and took a deep breath.

As he turned back to the battle, he saw something that made him shudder. Standing at the bow of a dark ship with skulls covering the black sails and cruel-looking iron workings on the railings, Mike saw the evil creature Sitnaw. He was surrounded by a cloud of darkness and shadow, and his mouth was forming words that Mike could not hear. As he spoke, part of the black cloud surrounding him floated over to Joshua's ships, covering many of the people.

They reacted very badly to these dark clouds, shivering and quaking with fear. They wept and fell to the ground, crying out, "It's hopeless! Ahh!"

Just as Mike looked up, one of the black clouds came toward his ship, and he was enveloped in it. He looked over at the enemy ship and watched in horror as Sitnaw grew to ten times his original size. Mike collapsed onto the deck and could not breathe, while waves of hopelessness and despair crashed over him. He felt sick to his stomach, unable to move.

Then he remembered Herald's words. *"Discouragement, despair, and hopelessness are some of his tactics. If you're not alert you'll think they're your own feelings and thoughts. Remember—keep alert."*

Taking a deep breath and struggling back onto his feet, Mike called out, "Joshua, help me!"

In an instant, Joshua appeared beside him and placed his hand on Mike's head. As the dark fog lifted, Mike watched Sitnaw shrink back to his ordinary size. Deep inside, he knew Sitnaw couldn't win against the authority and power that Joshua and his father possessed.

Joshua turned to Mike. "Few people from your world know what's taking place now."

Mike watched as creatures from Joshua's realm fought side by side with people from his own world who had sworn allegiance to Joshua and his father.

He and Mari went with Joshua from ship to ship, encouraging the troops and letting each person know that the prince was fighting with them. Many were seriously wounded, but when Joshua touched them, they stood up again, totally healed in mind and body, able to fight again.

Now he turned and looked at Mike and Mari. "What I'm about to do will make you very sad, but you must trust me."

Mike looked over at Mari and saw tears in her eyes. He was already feeling overwhelmed by the fighting all around him, and he felt a heaviness descend. Joshua continued.

"My father and I have a plan. It will all work out in the end. Have faith in me and do not fear." He put an arm around each of them. "Don't lose hope. Know that I will be with you again soon. Encourage those on the other ships when I am gone."

"When you're gone?" Tears filled Mari's eyes.

They both hugged Joshua tightly. "Please be careful. Don't do anything dangerous!" Mari sobbed.

He looked at them with such sadness in his eyes that Mike stepped back. Mari, visibly shaken, shuddered and sat down on the wooden decking at her feet.

Surprisingly, Joshua stepped off the ship and floated over to Sitnaw's vessel. Mike waited to see how Joshua would destroy the evil creature and those aboard his ship. But Joshua did nothing. He just stood there with his arms outstretched in the sign of surrender.

Sitnaw and his minions howled in victory as they surrounded Joshua and began to beat him with cruel weapons, tearing into his flesh. Mike put his hands over his ears to block out the shrieks of delight coming from the enemy ship as they tied Joshua onto the mast. Then a dark mist covered all the ships, and Mike could no longer see Joshua. A deep darkness continued to swallow up everything in its gloomy grip.

Mike put his arm around Mari and helped her to her feet. "Don't worry. It'll work out somehow." His words were lost in the noise of battle, and he felt a deep foreboding, wishing he were anywhere but on that ship.

As they waited, thunder clouds

threatened to release a torrent of rain;
then there was silence. Mike looked up
at the sky as darkness deepened into
night and the rain began to fall.

He and Mari stood in the down-
pour. Then a crack opened up in the
gloom, and they could see Joshua
surrounded by Sitnaw and many evil-
looking creatures who were beating
him cruelly.

Joshua looked across the water
that separated the two ships and into
Mike's eyes, forming a weak smile.
Then, Sitnaw's ship rapidly flooded
with water and sank like a stone into
the dark sea, taking everyone on it into
the depths below. Mike stood in
shocked silence as he watched every
evil ship sink into the stormy seas.

He couldn't believe his eyes.
What was Joshua thinking? How could
they win if he died?

"It's a mistake!" Mike fought back tears. He turned toward Mari, whose face looked pale. "It's over. He was our only hope, and now he's gone."

Mari looked out to sea. "Wasn't there another way?" She sighed deeply.

"It'll be all right. One thing that came from his death was all the enemy's ships went down with him...and Sitnaw."

Mari nodded sadly. "Better go see if we can help the others."

With heaviness of heart and drooping shoulders, Mike moved from ship to ship with Mari by his side, checking for the wounded and offering encouraging words. A deep sense of defeat and sorrow filled the night air.

Everyone gathered on the shore, setting up camp, and talking in whispers about the prince and all the kind things he had done for them. They shared stories well into the night, and as Mike listened, he wondered what would happen now.

Chapter Eight

A New Dawn

Early the next morning Mike woke up to Mari standing over him, looking radiant. Last night, her eyes had been red and swollen from crying and wiping the tears on her dirty sweatshirt. This morning, her eyes were clear, and her face was glowing.

She stood over his sleeping bag, holding her finger to her lips and waved him to follow her.

"It's too early. Go back to bed." He yawned.

She insisted, so he got out of his warm sleeping bag reluctantly and followed her quietly so as not to wake anyone in the camp.

The morning air was crisp and fresh, and the sunrise filled the sky with streaks of red and pink. That was one thing Mike loved about camping— being out in nature and waking up to the fresh air under an open sky.

He turned to Mari. "You look better today!"

"That's 'cause last night I had the

most peaceful dream. Joshua was in it. Can we walk a little and talk about it?"

"Sure." Mike walked beside her along the beach.

"Last night, after you fell asleep, Herald talked about the importance of dreams and to pay special attention to them." She stopped walking and looked at Mike. "Well, I think my dream last night was from Joshua."

Mike sat down on the cold sand, and Mari plopped down beside him. Her face glowed.

"Go on. I'm listening." Mike fought back a yawn.

"In my dream, Joshua was alive, and he wanted me to know every-thing's okay."

"Hmmm, don't get your hopes up. It's just a dream." Mike jumped up, deciding he needed to walk or he might doze off again.

They continued along the beach, arriving at a small, shaded cove still sleepy with the dew of morning. As they entered the sheltered bay, the sun was rising, filling the cove with beautiful, golden rays of sunshine.

There, sitting on a rock with a stick in his hand, was a man. He held a box of donuts in his lap, while bacon and sausage sizzled on an outdoor fire. Delicious smells raced to Mike's empty stomach, and he stopped to breathe in the aroma. The stranger looked up and smiled. He had the kindest eyes, and Mike immediately felt safe. There was something familiar about him.

The man pointed at the food. "If you're hungry, help yourself. There's plenty." He got up and handed the box of donuts to Mike.

"Thanks, I am hungry." Mike took the box and sat down with Mari on a rock next to the man.

Just being near the stranger brought comfort to both of them, and they felt their sorrows fading away. Mike found it peaceful to sit and look out at the beautiful ocean, watching the sunrise dancing on the water.

The man got up to leave.

"Can we walk with you?" Mike jumped up.

Mari stood.

"All right." The man waited for them.

As they joined him they shared the sad things that had taken place, especially the war and Joshua's death.

The stranger smiled at them. "Everything will end up all right. Trust me."

Mike and Mari looked at him and then at each other. "Joshua?"

That's why he had looked so

familiar. It was Joshua. They almost knocked him over in a double bear hug. The three of them embraced and laughed.

Mike got up from the hug and stared in disbelief at Joshua. Why hadn't he recognized him? He looked the same, and yet something had changed. "How'd you do it? We saw you sink with Sitnaw's ship." He took Joshua's hand to examine it.

Joshua turned and looked deep into Mike's and Mari's eyes. "Do you think any evil can destroy me? My father and I have completely disman- tled and destroyed the enemy's power."

He took Mari's hand. "Anyone who chooses to become part of my kingdom and trusts in me will be free from the enemy's evil."

"Oh, Joshua, that's wonderful.

You're alive." Mari squeezed his hand and laughed.

"The power I have over the enemy, I now give to you. Go tell your friends, family, and even strangers who will listen to you. Tell them that life will be different for anyone who becomes my friend."

Mike felt excitement welling up within him. If the king could bring his own son back to life after they'd seen him die, what else might he do?

He turned to Mari. "Now Joshua's back, anything can happen."

Mari laughed.

The small group walked toward the campsite, holding hands, Mari on one side of Joshua and Mike on the other.

Mari looked up into Joshua's face. "Everything's going to be different now that you're here."

Joshua smiled back at her. "And I'll never leave you."

Mike felt safe, happy, and excited, as he realized everything had changed on his world, now that Joshua was back. He smiled, thinking of all the new adventures that lay in store for them.

Look for the other books in this
series on Amazon.com

The Old Tree Series
Tricia Martin

Sheneau Stanley Pastor
livingfreeministries.org

Tricia, uses stories to share valuable life lessons and underlying important values that kids must have to have successful lives today.

R. Gutierrez

The Old Tree is a portal into a kingdom where courage, hope and the promise of a new day reminds one of love's enduring presence.

Desi d'Amani Artist

Enter the world of imagination, intrigue, and adventure! Whether young or younger still the Old
Tree is a door into a mystical adventure where life
isn't always as it appears to be and lessons are
learned through overcoming.

This book invites children to explore how
decisions affect the world around and beyond
them and it allows the childlike to re-embrace the
realities of the once real but forgotten invisible
realm. Step through the door into an adventure
that will cause you to rethink the world as you
once perceived it.

The Old Tree Series may very well be like a Chroni-
cles of Narnia for this generation.

Christy Peters Filmmaker

Love this book. The story takes the reader on an incredible adventure. I love how Tricia was able to incorporate things from the extra-terrestrial (spirit realm) and show how they can be just as real and merged into the lives of those of us who live on the terrestrial plain. Well done and an enjoyable read for child or adult!

Now available in paperback and e-book

The second book in
The Old Tree Series

The Land of Bizia

Tricia Martin

A VERY BUSY LAND

The Old Tree…a doorway to a busy land, an evil lord, beautiful, underground caverns, and a sinister plan waiting to be discovered.

Mike and Mari find themselves in a world that's on the verge of destroying itself through busyness. With the help of their loving and powerful friend, Joshua, can they rescue the people of Bizia and bring them back to the values, peace, and fun they once knew?

Now available in paperback and e-book

The third book in
The Old Tree Series

The Kingdom of Knon

Tricia Martin

AN UNDERWATER KINGDOM IN CHAOS

The Old Tree…a doorway to an underwater kingdom in chaos, a beautiful princess needing to be rescued…a book that holds the key.

The Book has been stolen! That rare gift from the Creator to the people of the Kingdom of Knon when first their kingdom had been made. Now everything has changed in Princess Aria's beautiful kingdom, and confusion, chaos, and fear rule her land.

Joshua brings Mike and Mari to the underwater kingdom to join with Princess Aria. Together, they must travel into space to defeat evil Sitnaw's plan to rule the Kingdom of Knon.

Now available in paperback and e-book

The fourth book in

The Old Tree Series

The Mild, Mild West

Tricia Martin

A GHOST TOWN AWAITS

The Old Tree…a doorway to a ghost town, talking quail, and evil Sitnaw prowling around a town of innocent families.

Mike and Mari arrive in the middle of the night in front of the Old Tree where Joshua is waiting. They join Mie, a member of a race of warrior beings from Joshua's realm, and journey into an Old West town to help in an important rescue. Young people have been suddenly disappearing from their families. Mike, Mari, Mie and Joshua join a group of quail who are eager to defeat the sinister plans of Sitnaw.

Now available in paperback and e-book

The fifth book in
The Old Tree Series

Into the Night Sky

Tricia Martin

A FLIGHT INTO SPACE

The Old Tree…a voyage into space in a
horse-drawn carriage…a search for a
special hat…a temptation.

Mike and Mari befriend a British boy, and all three
find themselves in the middle of the night on Philip's
street. On Philip's front lawn is a carriage attached to
two fiery horses waiting to fly them into space to
search for an extraordinary hat that has been stolen
from the land of Bizia.

Now available in paperback and e-book

The sixth book in
The Old Tree Series

Arabian Lights

Tricia Martin

JOURNEY TO A BARREN DESERT LAND

The Old Tree...a doorway to a barren desert...a band of thieves...an oasis...a lost baby.

Mari's father and his sister, as children, discovered the old tree for the first time. When they walk through the other side, they find themselves in a barren desert. An important child needs their help to restore his purpose.

Now available in paperback and e-book

The seventh book in
The Old Tree Series

One For All and All for One

Tricia Martin

LANDS AND KINGDOMS IN PERIL

The Old Tree…where they travel through time…Abe Lincoln shows up as a child…hope is lost, and they must restore it.

All the worlds, lands, and kingdoms are on the verge of being destroyed by evil Sitnaw. Joshua asks Mike and Mari to travel back in time to solve this problem. They must find Abe Lincoln when he was a child and convince him to join with them to prevent the destruction of all they value.

After raising her own child, Tricia Martin now desires to impact the hearts of children with her fantasy adventures involving a loving, kind, and powerful God who transforms the lives of all that come into contact with Him. She has a Master of Arts in counseling and belongs to the Society of Children's Book Writers and Illustrators, SCBWI.

She has a passion to see children introduced to wholesome reading and believes books feed the mind the way food feeds the body. The reader joins in transforming lands and kingdoms that have been ravaged by the enemy. The reader will fly into space, swim down to an underwater kingdom, travel to the Wild West, visit a desert, and enjoy many other adventures. Each book has educational aspects that parents or grand-parents can study with their children.